Disney's DARKWING DUCK

THE SILLY CANINE CAPER

By Justine Korman
Illustrated by Don Williams

A GOLDEN BOOK • NEW YORK

Western Publishing Company, Inc., Racine, Wisconsin 53404

Darkwing and his sidekick, Launchpad McQuack, had just been called to the headquarters of the famous spy organization S.H.U.S.H. While the two of them waited to hear about their next mission, Launchpad danced to a tune on his Duckman radio.

"Launchpad, stop that wacky wiggling!" Darkwing snapped. "Do you always have to be so silly?"

As Launchpad pulled off his headphones, he knocked a stack of papers off the desk.

Bending to pick them up, he then bumped into the fishbowl, spilling it all over S.H.U.S.H. leader J. Gander Hooter, who was just walking in the door.

"Launchpad, that does it!" screamed Darkwing. "No more stumbling sidekick. From now on, I, Darkwing Duck, scourge of evil, will fly solo!"

Launchpad left the office feeling sad. But instead of leaving the building, he listened secretly from the hall.

"Here's the problem, Darkwing," said Hooter, heaving a sigh. "Agents all over the world are forgetting their missions, even their names! They're all turning . . . silly!"

"Who could be behind this putrid prank?" Darkwing wondered aloud.

"Our only clue is this robot puppy," Hooter explained as he showed Darkwing a photograph of the robot. "We've discovered that these dogs send out a Silly Signal that turns our agents into idiots. You've got to track down one of these dogs and find out who's controlling them," the chief continued. "Luckily, we've invented a gadget to help you."

Darkwing quickly went over to the S.H.U.S.H. laboratory
to see the new invention, which was disguised to look like
an ordinary cape.

"It can track robot pups and protect you from the Silly
Signal," the S.H.U.S.H. inventor explained.

"Purple—my favorite color!" Darkwing said as he swirled
his new cape. "Let's get dangerous!" he exclaimed.

"Look! A blip on my cape's radar screen," said Darkwing excitedly. "Time for the feathered avenger to get flapping!"

"Wait!" the inventor called after Darkwing. "I haven't shown you how all the switches work!"

But the daring duck was already following the blip to . . .

. . . J. Gander Hooter's office! Darkwing found the chief
of the world's greatest secret intelligence agency sitting on
the floor, cutting out a chain of paper ducks.

"Yap! Yap!" barked a robot puppy as it zoomed from the room. Darkwing raced after it.

"Darkwing Duck pursues the metallic mutt!" he called out as he ran. "My mission—to save all S.H.U.S.H. agents from certain silliness!"

Roaring along on the Ratcatcher, Darkwing tracked the puppy to an abandoned dog chow factory. On tiptoe, Darkwing then followed the robot pup through a back door of the factory.

The dedicated detective did not notice that he was being followed, too!

"It's the monstrous Madam Anna Matronic!" muttered
Darkwing. "She and her computerized critters are behind
this sinister scheme!"

From his hiding place, he watched Madam Matronic toss
a battery yummy to the puppy that had just returned. "Good
work, Muttmatic. Good dog," said the computer whiz.

Darkwing looked around and gasped. "This entire factory is filled with computer puppies, ready to turn every good guy into a giggling goof!

"I've got to stop her! But first, my cape . . ." Darkwing fumbled with the switches on his cape, trying to remember which one would protect him from the Silly Signal. He wanted to catch Madam Matronic—not wind up as another dumb duck.

Darkwing flipped the wrong switch and suddenly his cape blasted rock music from a radio station. The robot puppies bopped happily to the beat.

"Stop dancing, you dogs!" shouted Madam Matronic. "Grab that duck!"

Darkwing reached for his gas gun, but it was too late!
Before he could say, "Down, doggies!" a dozen steel jaws
clamped onto his cape.

Madam Matronic tied Darkwing to a table and aimed her Silly Signal ray gun right at the tip of his beak.

"Wait!" Darkwing pleaded. "At least tell me why you invented the Silly Signal!"

"I was trying to make my robot critters smarter," the scientist admitted. "But my experiments backfired! My robots became totally silly, instead. Then I realized I had the perfect weapon. I could turn all the S.H.U.S.H. agents into helpless twits!

"How nice of you to waddle right into my hideout, Darkwing," Madam Matronic said with a snicker.

Darkwing closed his eyes and braced himself for an express ride to the zany zone.

Just as Madam Matronic fired the Silly Signal, someone leaped from the shadows and shielded Darkwing from the ray's blast.

"Launchpad!" cried Darkwing.

Madam Matronic stared at Launchpad. "Why isn't he getting silly?" she asked with a look of panic in her eyes.

Darkwing laughed. "Maybe it doesn't work on someone who's already silly."

"No one is *that* silly," the scientist declared. Frantically, she began to examine her ray gun. Then she accidentally blasted herself!

Madam Matronic began to giggle. "Now which puppy-wuppy wants another battery yummy?" she asked, skipping off to play with her dogs.

"Launchpad, you were great!" Darkwing exclaimed. "How did you do it?"

"Simple! I blocked the Silly Signal by turning on my radio headphones." Launchpad danced around as he explained, knocking into a table of glass beakers.

"You're a dunce of a dancer," said Darkwing with a laugh. "But you're a pretty perfect partner!"

Back at S.H.U.S.H. headquarters, J. Gander Hooter was his old self again. He congratulated both agents on a job well done.

"As you can tell," Hooter concluded, "the lab finally found a cure for the Silly Signal. Everything is back to normal.

"Well," he added with a silly grin, "everything except my office!"